WOULD YOU RATHER?
FOR
TEENS!

Includes a BONUS

EWW! YUCK! GROSS!

chapter at the end of this book!

HILARIOUS AND FUN!

RatherFunnyPress.com

Books By
RATHER FUNNY PRESS

Would You Rather? For 6 Year Old Kids!
Would You Rather? For 7 Year Old Kids!
Would You Rather? For 8 Year Old Kids!
Would You Rather? For 9 Year Old Kids!
Would You Rather? For 10 Year Old Kids!
Would You Rather? For 11 Year Old Kids!
Would You Rather? For 12 Year Old Kids!
Would You Rather? For Teens!
Would You Rather? Eww! Yuck! Gross!

To see all the latest books by
Rather Funny Press just go to
RatherFunnyPress.com

RatherFunnyPress.com

YOUR FREE SURPRISE GIFT!

HILARIOUS JOKES FOR CLEVER KIDS!

RATHER FUNNY PRESS

Details on the last page of this book!
A brand new free joke book
just for you.
Check it out! Laughter awaits!

RatherFunnyPress.com

HOW TO PLAY

This easy to play game is a ton of fun!
Have 2 or more players.
The first reader will choose a 'Would You Rather?'
from the book and read it aloud.
The other player(s) then choose which scenario
they would prefer and why.
You can't say 'neither' or 'none'.
You must choose one and explain why.
Then the book is passed to the next person
and the game continues!

The main rule is have fun, laugh and enjoy
spending time with your friends and family.
Let the fun begin!

ATTENTION!

All the scenarios and choices in this book are
fictional and meant to be about using your
imagination, having a ton of fun and enjoying this
game with your friends and family.
Obviously, DO NOT ATTEMPT any of these
scenarios in real life.

RatherFunnyPress.com

WOULD YOU RATHER...

BE FORCED TO DANCE EVERY TIME YOU HEARD MUSIC

OR

FORCED TO SING ALONG TO ANY SONG YOU HEARD?

MAKE REALLY LOUD BURPS THAT DON'T SMELL

OR

VERY QUIET BURPS THAT SMELL REALLY BAD?

WOULD YOU RATHER...

GIVE UP YOUR CELL PHONE
FOR 6 MONTHS

OR

LOSE ONE OF YOUR FRIENDS
FOREVER?

BATTLE A TURKEY THE SIZE
OF A GIRAFFE

OR

20 GIRAFFES THE SIZE
OF A TURKEY?

WOULD YOU RATHER...

CUDDLE AN ANGRY CHICKEN

OR

A RELAXED LION?

WAKE UP AS A NEW RANDOM PERSON EVERY YEAR

OR

SPEND A DAY INSIDE A STRANGER WITHOUT HAVING ANY CONTROL OVER THEM?

WOULD YOU RATHER...

HAVE EYES THAT CHANGE COLOR DEPENDING ON YOUR MOOD

OR

HAIR THAT CHANGES COLOR DEPENDING ON THE WEATHER?

HAVE A 3D PRINTER YOU CAN USE ALL THE TIME

OR

THE BEST CELL PHONE YOU CAN GET?

WOULD YOU RATHER...

SURF IN SHARK-INFESTED
WATERS

OR

PARACHUTE INTO THE
GRAND CANYON?

EAT A LIVE SCORPION

OR

DRINK MUDDY WATER?

WOULD YOU RATHER...

BE A CHARACTER IN YOUR
FAVORITE VIDEO GAME

OR

A CHARACTER IN YOUR
FAVORITE MOVIE?

NIBBLE ON YOUR PHONE
FOR AN HOUR

OR

EAT 2 BOXES OF TISSUES
IN AN HOUR?

WOULD YOU RATHER...

KNOW THE HISTORY OF EVERY OBJECT YOU TOUCHED

OR

BE ABLE TO TALK TO ANIMALS?

HAVE TWO TONGUES

OR

NO TONGUE AT ALL?

WOULD YOU RATHER...

LOOK LIKE YOUR GRANDPA

OR

SMELL LIKE YOUR GRANDPA?

BE ABLE TO MAKE YOUR FAVORITE FOODS MAGICALLY APPEAR

OR

YOUR LEAST FAVORITE FOODS DISAPPEAR INTO THIN AIR?

WOULD YOU RATHER...

EAT FAST FOOD BURGERS
EVERY NIGHT

OR

CHINESE TAKE-OUT
EVERY NIGHT?

BE REALLY HEALTHY FOR THE
REST OF YOUR LIFE

OR

REALLY WEALTHY FOR THE
REST OF YOUR LIFE?

WOULD YOU RATHER...

COUNT TO 1,000 AND
RECEIVE $1,000

OR

COUNT TO 1,000,000 AND
RECEIVE ONE WISH?

RECEIVE ONE VALENTINE'S DAY
CARD AND KNOW WHO SENT IT

OR

RECEIVE 3 VALENTINE'S DAY
CARDS BUT NOT KNOW WHO
THEY'RE FROM?

WOULD YOU RATHER...

HAVE YOUR GRANDPARENTS PICK WHO YOU MARRY

OR

BE SINGLE FOREVER?

BE ALLERGIC TO PEANUT BUTTER

OR

ALLERGIC TO ICE CREAM?

WOULD YOU RATHER...

BE WITHOUT ANY EARS

OR

BE WITHOUT ANY FINGERS?

HAVE THE POWER OF INVISIBILITY

OR

BE ABLE TO LIVE FOREVER AND NEVER GET OLD?

WOULD YOU RATHER...

SIT WITH A RESTING TIGER
FOR TEN MINUTES

OR

RUN ACROSS A HUNGRY
ALLIGATOR'S BACK?

HAVE UNLIMITED
INTERNATIONAL FIRST-CLASS
PLANE TICKETS

OR

NEVER HAVE TO PAY FOR FOOD
AT RESTAURANTS AGAIN?

WOULD YOU RATHER...

BE IN JAIL FOR A YEAR

OR

LOSE A YEAR OFF YOUR LIFE?

DANCE IN FRONT OF 1,000 PEOPLE

OR

SING IN FRONT OF 1,000 PEOPLE?

WOULD YOU RATHER...

HAVE A SQUEAKY HIGH PITCHED VOICE

OR

A REALLY DEEP AND LOUD VOICE?

GIVE UP WATCHING TV AND MOVIES FOR A YEAR

OR

GIVE UP VIDEO GAMES FOR A YEAR?

WOULD YOU RATHER...

TELL THE TRUTH AND NOBODY BELIEVED YOU

OR

TELL LIES AND EVERYONE BELIEVED YOU?

HAVE A JOB YOU DON'T LIKE MAKING $100,000 A YEAR

OR

HAVE A JOB YOU LOVE AND MAKE $30,000 A YEAR?

WOULD YOU RATHER...

HAVE ALL TRAFFIC LIGHTS YOU APPROACH TURN GREEN

OR

NEVER HAVE TO STAND IN LINE AGAIN?

MOVE TO A NEW CITY OR TOWN EVERY WEEK

OR

NEVER BE ABLE TO LEAVE THE CITY OR TOWN YOU WERE BORN IN?

WOULD YOU RATHER...

NEVER BE ABLE TO LEAVE YOUR OWN COUNTRY

OR

NEVER BE ABLE TO FLY IN AN AIRPLANE?

LIVE IN THE WILDERNESS FOR THE REST OF YOUR LIFE

OR

HAVE NO LEGS?

WOULD YOU RATHER...

BE COMPLETELY INSANE AND KNOW THAT YOU ARE INSANE

OR

COMPLETELY INSANE AND BELIEVE YOU ARE SANE?

GO BOWLING WITH YOUR FAVORITE CELEBRITY

OR

THE PRESIDENT?

WOULD YOU RATHER...

GO WITHOUT MUSIC FOR THE
REST OF YOUR LIFE

OR

HAVE NO TV FOR A YEAR?

HAVE TO PEE EVERY
HOUR

OR

POOP EVERY HOUR?

WOULD YOU RATHER...

BE ABLE TO DODGE ANYTHING
NO MATTER HOW FAST
IT'S MOVING

OR

BE ABLE TO ASK ANY THREE
QUESTIONS AND HAVE THEM
ANSWERED TRUTHFULLY?

MEET SOMEONE WHO HAS
THREE EYES ON THEIR
FOREHEAD

OR

TWO MOUTHS?

WOULD YOU RATHER...

WAKE UP WITH
KITTEN PAWS

OR

A GIANT MOUSE TAIL?

BE IN A MESSY
FOOD FIGHT

OR

WATCH THE FOOD FIGHT
FROM AFAR?

WOULD YOU RATHER...

EAT A SPOONFUL OF
FRIED INSECTS

OR

A SPOONFUL OF EXTREMELY
SPICY HOT SAUCE?

FACE AN ARMY OF GRANDMAS
WITH KNITTING NEEDLES

OR

AN ARMY OF GRANDPAS
ARMED WITH SPOONS?

WOULD YOU RATHER...

HAVE ONE HAND WITH
8 FINGERS

OR

ONE FOOT WITH 8 TOES?

CREATE A NEW
BESTSELLING APP

OR

BE A FAMOUS YOUTUBE STAR?

WOULD YOU RATHER...

LOSE YOUR ARMS

OR

YOUR TOES?

BE AN AVERAGE PERSON IN THE PRESENT

OR

A KING OR QUEEN OF A LARGE COUNTRY 800 YEARS AGO?

WOULD YOU RATHER...

BE LOST IN THE WOODS
AT NIGHT

OR

STUCK IN A HAUNTED
HOUSE AT NIGHT?

DANCE AROUND YOUR HOUSE
IN YOUR UNDERWEAR

OR

DANCE AROUND THE
NEIGHBOURHOOD WEARING YOUR
UNDERWEAR AS A HAT?

WOULD YOU RATHER...

OWN AN OLD-TIME PIRATE SHIP WITH CREW

OR

A PRIVATE JET WITH A PILOT AND INFINITE FUEL?

HAVE A MULTICOLORED HEAD

OR

A TWO FOOT LONG TAIL?

WOULD YOU RATHER...

EAT ALL YOUR MEALS
FROZEN

OR

ALL YOUR MEALS ARE
SUPER SALTY?

HAVE EDIBLE SPAGHETTI HAIR
THAT REGROWS EVERY NIGHT

OR

SWEAT MAPLE SYRUP?

WOULD YOU RATHER...

HAVE THE HEAD OF AN
80 YEAR OLD

OR

THE HEAD OF A NEW
BORN BABY?

MAKE A HOUSE OUT OF
ICE CREAM

OR

A FORT OUT OF CHEESE?

WOULD YOU RATHER...

GET $5 EVERY TIME YOU EAT AN APPLE

OR

$1 EVERY TIME YOU EAT A BIG MAC?

NEVER USE SOCIAL MEDIA SITES/APPS AGAIN

OR

NEVER WATCH ANOTHER MOVIE OR TV SHOW?

WOULD YOU RATHER...

HAVE EVERYTHING YOU DRAW BECOME REAL BUT BE TERRIBLE AT DRAWING

OR

BE ABLE TO FLY BUT ONLY AS FAST AS YOU CAN WALK?

HAVE AWESOME NINJA SKILLS

OR

HAVE AMAZING CODING SKILLS IN ANY COMPUTER LANGUAGE?

WOULD YOU RATHER...

HAVE AN EASY JOB WORKING FOR SOMEONE ELSE

OR

WORK FOR YOURSELF BUT WORK INCREDIBLY HARD?

HAVE ONE HAND TWICE AS BIG AS USUAL

OR

HALF THE USUAL SIZE?

WOULD YOU RATHER...

JUMP INTO A POOL OF MELTED CHOCOLATE

OR

A HOT TUB OF VANILLA ICE CREAM?

HAVE A BOOK THAT TELLS YOU EVERYTHING THAT WILL HAPPEN IN THE FUTURE

OR

A BOOK THAT TELLS YOU EVERYTHING THAT ALREADY HAPPENED BUT WE DON'T KNOW ABOUT?

WOULD YOU RATHER...

HAVE EVERYTHING YOU EAT
BE TOO SALTY

OR

NOT SALTY ENOUGH NO MATTER
HOW MUCH SALT YOU ADD?

BE COMPELLED TO HIGH FIVE
EVERYONE YOU MEET

OR

GIVE WEDGIES TO ANYONE IN A
GREEN SHIRT?

WOULD YOU RATHER...

TAKE A CODING CLASS

OR

AN ART CLASS?

NEVER EAT CHOCOLATE AGAIN

OR

ONLY EAT CHOCOLATE WHEN IT'S COATING BRUSSEL SPROUTS?

WOULD YOU RATHER...

BE ABLE TO CONTROL FIRE

OR

WATER?

HAVE EARBUDS THAT NEVER SIT RIGHT IN YOUR EARS

OR

HAVE ALL MUSIC PLAYED VERY QUIETLY?

WOULD YOU RATHER...

BE GIVEN ONE MILLION DOLLARS THAT YOU HAVE TO SPEND IN A WEEK

OR

TEN THOUSAND DOLLARS A MONTH FOR THE REST OF YOUR LIFE?

BE ABLE TO CREATE PORTALS

OR

CONTROL GRAVITY?

WOULD YOU RATHER...

SPEND THE REST OF YOUR DAYS IN A SUBMARINE

OR

A HOT AIR BALLOON?

HAVE WHATEVER YOU ARE THINKING APPEAR ABOVE YOUR HEAD FOR EVERYONE TO SEE

OR

HAVE ABSOLUTELY EVERYTHING YOU DO LIVE STREAMED FOR ANYONE TO SEE?

WOULD YOU RATHER...

BE THE ONLY CHILD

OR

HAVE 4 BROTHERS AND SISTERS?

HAVE SKIN THAT CHANGES COLOR BASED ON YOUR EMOTIONS

OR

TATTOOS APPEAR ALL OVER YOUR BODY DEPICTING WHAT YOU DID YESTERDAY?

WOULD YOU RATHER...

GIVE UP BATHING FOR
A MONTH

OR

GIVE UP THE INTERNET FOR
A MONTH?

MOVE THINGS WITH
YOUR MIND

OR

READ PEOPLE'S MINDS?

WOULD YOU RATHER...

BE STUCK IN A STINKY TOILET
BECAUSE THE DOOR
WON'T OPEN

OR

HAVE TO USE A RESTROOM
TOILET THAT HAS NO DOOR?

THERE BE A PERPETUAL WATER
BALLOON WAR GOING ON
IN YOUR NEIGHBORHOOD

OR

A PERPETUAL FOOD FIGHT?

WOULD YOU RATHER...

HAVE A NEVER-ENDING SUPPLY OF CUPCAKES

OR

A NEVER-ENDING SUPPLY OF CHEESEBURGERS?

HAVE BOTH LEGS STUCK IN THE TOILET BOWL

OR

HAVE BOTH HANDS STUCK IN THE TOILET BOWL?

WOULD YOU RATHER...

VACATION IN ENGLAND

OR

VACATION IN GERMANY?

SPEAK EVERY LANGUAGE
EXCEPT ENGLISH

OR

UNDERSTAND ENGLISH BUT YOU
CAN ONLY RESPOND IN SIGN
LANGUAGE?

WOULD YOU RATHER...

NOT BE ALLOWED TO WASH YOUR HANDS FOR A MONTH

OR

YOUR HAIR FOR A MONTH?

HAVE A REALLY BIG, POWERFUL NOSE

OR

REALLY BIG, POWERFUL EARS?

WOULD YOU RATHER...

HAVE YOUR SKIN CHANGE COLOR EVERY 15 MINUTES

OR

YOUR EYES CHANGE COLOR EVERY 5 MINUTES?

DO THE CHICKEN DANCE IN FRONT OF YOUR FRIENDS

OR

IN A YOUTUBE VIDEO?

WOULD YOU RATHER...

SUDDENLY BE ELECTED A SENATOR

OR

SUDDENLY BECOME A CEO OF A MAJOR COMPANY?

NEVER HAVE TO WORK AGAIN

OR

NEVER HAVE TO SLEEP AGAIN?

WOULD YOU RATHER...

HAVE A UNICORN OF YOUR OWN THAT YOU CAN TALK TO

OR

BE A UNICORN YOURSELF?

BE YODA

OR

BABY YODA?

WOULD YOU RATHER...

INSTANTLY LEARN PIANO PERFECTLY

OR

GUITAR PERFECTLY?

HAVE A SMALL CHILD PEE THEIR PANTS WHILE SITTING ON YOUR LAP

OR

YOU PEE YOUR PANTS WHILE IN CLASS?

WOULD YOU RATHER...

COMPETE IN A RACE
AND LOSE

OR

NOT COMPETE BUT KNOW YOU
WOULD HAVE WON IF YOU DID?

HAVE ONE SONG OF YOUR
CHOICE PLAY ON REPEAT
24 HOURS A DAY FOR A WEEK

OR

HAVE SONGS THAT YOU HAVE
NO CONTROL OVER PLAY 24
HOURS A DAY FOR A MONTH?

WOULD YOU RATHER...

EAT PANCAKES FOR EVERY MEAL FOR A WEEK

OR

SPAGHETTI FOR EVERY MEAL FOR A MONTH?

BE ABLE TO CONTROL ELECTRONICS WITH YOUR MIND

OR

CONTROL ANIMALS (BUT NOT HUMANS) WITH YOUR MIND?

WOULD YOU RATHER...

BE ABLE TO SEE 10 MINUTES INTO YOUR OWN FUTURE

OR

10 MINUTES INTO THE FUTURE OF ANYONE BUT YOURSELF?

HAVE AN INSTANT PORTAL TO A PIZZERIA

OR

THE MALL?

WOULD YOU RATHER...

HAVE OUT OF CONTROL
BODY HAIR

OR

A STRONG, PUNGENT
BODY ODOR?

HAVE A BUBBLE GUN THAT
MAKES 6 FOOT BUBBLES THAT
LAST FOR 5 MINUTES

OR

A 6 FEET HIGH
PILE OF LEGOS?

WOULD YOU RATHER...

EAT A PIECE OF GUM YOU FOUND ON THE STREET

OR

GIVE YOUR ALREADY CHEWED GUM TO SOMEONE YOU JUST MET?

HAVE TO USE A FILTHY RESTROOM TOILET

OR

A SPARKLING CLEAN TOILET THAT HAS A SNAKE IN IT?

WOULD YOU RATHER...

HAVE A BABY THROW UP ON YOU

OR

YOU THROW UP ON A BABY?

STAY THE AGE YOU ARE NOW UNTIL YOU TURN 70

OR

INSTANTLY TURN 40 AND STAY 40 FOR THE REST OF YOUR LIFE?

WOULD YOU RATHER...

HAVE MILK LEAK FROM YOUR NOSE EVERY TIME YOU LAUGHED

OR

CRY MILK FROM YOUR EYES EVERY TIME YOU SNEEZED?

HAVE BABY SNAKES FOR HAIR

OR

ADULT SNAKES FOR ARMS?

WOULD YOU RATHER...

BE STUCK IN AN AQUARIUM WITH A GREAT WHITE SHARK

OR

IN A ROOM WHERE THE FLOOR IS COVERED BY SPIDERS?

TELL YOUR MOST EMBARRASSING SECRET TO ALL YOUR FRIENDS

OR

EAT 500 LIQUORICE JELLY BEANS IN ONE HOUR?

WOULD YOU RATHER...

HAVE A FOOD FIGHT AGAINST YOUR PARENTS

OR

YOUR GRANDPARENTS?

VISIT THE INTERNATIONAL SPACE STATION FOR A WEEK

OR

STAY IN AN UNDERWATER HOTEL FOR A WEEK?

WOULD YOU RATHER...

HAVE YOUR GRANDMOTHER'S HAIRSTYLE

OR

YOUR GRANDMOTHER'S FIRST NAME?

HAVE MULTICOLORED EYEBROWS

OR

BRIGHT GREEN EYEBROWS?

WOULD YOU RATHER...

LIVE IN A FOREIGN PLACE AND NOT KNOW THE LANGUAGE

OR

LIVE ON AN ISLAND ALONE?

HAVE EMBARRASSING PICTURES OF YOU SENT TO YOUR EX

OR

YOUR TEACHER?

WOULD YOU RATHER...

LIVE IN THE SKY IN A FLOATING APARTMENT

OR

LIVE UNDERWATER IN A PARKED SUBMARINE?

SPEND THE NIGHT IN A SMALL ROWBOAT IN SHARK INFESTED WATERS

OR

ON A SMALL RAFT IN AN ALLIGATOR INFESTED SWAMP?

WOULD YOU RATHER...

THE FLOOR OF YOUR ROOM
IS A BED

OR

HAVE A TRAMPOLINE ON
THE ROOF?

HOLD A HEDGEHOG

OR

KISS A WARTY TOAD?

WOULD YOU RATHER...

BE LOST IN THE WOODS AND HAVE TWO ITEMS OF YOUR CHOICE

OR

ONE PERSON OF YOUR CHOICE?

BE IN YOUR FAVORITE VIDEO GAME

OR

YOUR FAVORITE TV SHOW?

WOULD YOU RATHER...

MEET A HORSE THAT WALKS
ON TWO LEGS

OR

A HORSE THAT TALKS?

HAVE CUTE FLOPPY EARS
LIKE A DOG

OR

A LONG TAIL LIKE A
MONKEY?

WOULD YOU RATHER...

BECOME FIVE YEARS OLDER

OR

BECOME TWO YEARS YOUNGER?

DRINK A GLASS OF MUSTARD IN ONE SITTING

OR

USE MUSTARD AS TOOTHPASTE FOR THE NEXT 3 WEEKS?

WOULD YOU RATHER...

LOSE YOUR BEST FRIEND

OR

ALL OF YOUR FRIENDS EXCEPT FOR YOUR BEST FRIEND?

GIVE UP ALL DRINKS EXCEPT FOR WATER

OR

GIVE UP EATING ANYTHING THAT WAS COOKED IN AN OVEN?

WOULD YOU RATHER...

INVITE BABY YODA TO A DINNER PARTY AT YOUR HOUSE

OR

JESUS TO A DINNER PARTY AT YOUR HOUSE?

BE FORCED TO ATTEND SCHOOL FOR YOUR WHOLE LIFE

OR

ONLY BE ABLE TO EAT GREEN VEGETABLES?

WOULD YOU RATHER...

HAVE A FULL SUIT OF ARMOR YOU CAN WEAR ANYTIME

OR

HAVE A HORSE YOU CAN RIDE ANYTIME?

TRAVEL THE WORLD FOR A YEAR ON A SHOESTRING BUDGET

OR

STAY IN ONLY ONE COUNTRY FOR A YEAR BUT LIVE IN LUXURY?

WOULD YOU RATHER...

TAKE A SELFIE WITH THE PRESIDENT

OR

THE QUEEN?

EVERY SINGLE THING YOU ATE FROM NOW ON TASTED LIKE KFC

OR

CHOCOLATE?

WOULD YOU RATHER...

HAVE A PET RAT THAT CAN SPEAK ENGLISH

OR

A PET RABBIT THAT IS BIG ENOUGH TO RIDE?

BE UNABLE TO USE SEARCH ENGINES

OR

UNABLE TO USE SOCIAL MEDIA?

WOULD YOU RATHER...

HAVE A PET DRAGON THAT YOU HAVE TRAINED

OR

BE SOMEONE ELSE'S PET DRAGON THAT THEY TRAINED?

HAVE UNLIMITED PEPSI

OR

UNLIMITED VEGAN CHOCOLATE?

WOULD YOU RATHER...

SURVIVE A PLANE CRASH
IN THE DESERT

OR

AN AVALANCHE IN
THE MOUNTAINS?

HAVE THE HEAD OF YOUR
TEACHER WITH YOUR BODY

OR

THE BODY OF YOUR TEACHER
WITH YOUR HEAD?

WOULD YOU RATHER...

BE A GIANT RABBIT

OR

A MINIATURE ELEPHANT?

BE LOCKED INSIDE A SCARY LIBRARY AT NIGHT

OR

AN OLD MUSEUM AT NIGHT?

WOULD YOU RATHER...

BE BEAUTIFUL/HANDSOME
BUT STUPID

OR

INTELLIGENT BUT UGLY?

ACTUALLY HAVE TO LAUGH OUT
LOUD EVERY TIME YOU
TYPE LOL

OR

ALWAYS REPLICATE THE FACE
OF ANY EMOJI YOU USE?

WOULD YOU RATHER...

DISCOVER A NEW ELEMENT AND NAME IT AFTER YOURSELF

OR

WIN GOLD AT THE OLYMPIC GAMES?

EAT A BOWL OF SPAGHETTI NOODLES WITHOUT SAUCE

OR

A BOWL OF SPAGHETTI SAUCE WITHOUT NOODLES?

WOULD YOU RATHER...

HAVE A CUDDLE WITH A SMALL BEAR

OR

A LARGE COYOTE?

WEAR DARK SUNGLASSES ALL DAY AND NIGHT FOR A WEEK

OR

HUGE EARPHONES FOR A MONTH?

WOULD YOU RATHER...

EAT LIVE MAGGOTS

OR

POOP OUT LIVE MAGGOTS?

HAVE A BOWL OF ICE CREAM
FOR BREAKFAST

OR

A BOWL OF CHOCOLATE
FOR DINNER?

WOULD YOU RATHER...

GO SWIMMING IN A RIVER OF WARM COFFEE

OR

DIVE INTO A POOL OF MILK?

WIN A 1-DAY SHOPPING SPREE TO ANY STORE

OR

A 2-WEEK VACATION TO ANY DESTINATION?

WOULD YOU RATHER...

HAVE NO INTERNET FOR A MONTH

OR

NO CELL PHONE FOR A WEEK?

NEVER LOSE YOUR PHONE AGAIN

OR

YOUR KEYS AGAIN?

WOULD YOU RATHER...

YOU HAVE SUPER POWERS BUT THE GOVERNMENT EXPERIMENTS ON YOU

OR

YOU'RE TOTALLY NORMAL?

HAVE ONE REALLY GOOD FRIEND

OR

8 NOT SO GOOD FRIENDS?

WOULD YOU RATHER...

BE IN PRISON FOR
20 YEARS

OR

HAVE NO ARMS?

ALWAYS SPEAK ALL YOUR
THOUGHTS ALOUD

OR

NEVER SPEAK AT ALL
(NOT EVEN IN SIGN
LANGUAGE)?

WOULD YOU RATHER...

EAT 8 CELERY STICKS
EVERY DAY

OR

EAT A CAN OF BAKED BEANS
EVERY DAY?

HAVE A VERY MUSCULAR
LOWER BODY AND A NORMAL
UPPER BODY

OR

A MUSCULAR UPPER BODY AND
A VERY SKINNY LOWER BODY?

WOULD YOU RATHER...

HAVE A PARROT MAKE A NEST IN YOUR HAIR

OR

A SEAGULL LAY EGGS IN YOUR HAIR?

30 BUTTERFLIES APPEAR EVERY TIME YOU SNEEZE

OR

ONE VERY ANGRY SQUIRREL APPEARS EVERY TIME YOU COUGH?

WOULD YOU RATHER...

LIVE UNDER A SKY WITH NO STARS AT NIGHT

OR

NO CLOUDS DURING THE DAY?

SPEND THE REST OF YOUR LIFE WITH A YACHT AS YOUR HOME

OR

AN RV AS YOUR HOME?

WOULD YOU RATHER...

PARACHUTE OFF THE TOP OF THE EMPIRE STATE BUILDING

OR

RUN THE LENGTH OF THE GREAT WALL OF CHINA?

NEVER EAT VEGETABLES AGAIN BUT YOU CAN'T EAT CHOCOLATE

OR

EAT VEGETABLES WITH CHOCOLATE FOR BREAKFAST EVERY DAY?

WOULD YOU RATHER...

FIND YOUR TRUE LOVE

OR

A SUITCASE WITH ONE MILLION DOLLARS INSIDE?

HAVE BRIGHT BLUE SKIN

OR

REALLY BRIGHT WHITE SKIN?

WOULD YOU RATHER...

HAVE MULTICOLORED
STRIPED HAIR

OR

HAIR THAT TASTES
LIKE KFC?

A WEEK ON HOLIDAY WITH IRON
MAN BUT YOU CAN'T
TELL ANYONE

OR

2 HOURS WITH WONDER
WOMAN AND YOU'RE ALLOWED
TO TELL EVERYONE?

WOULD YOU RATHER...

LIVE IN THE BEST HOUSE IN THE WORST NEIGHBORHOOD

OR

THE WORST HOUSE IN THE BEST NEIGHBORHOOD?

HAVE ONE REAL GET OUT OF JAIL FREE CARD

OR

A KEY THAT OPENS ANY DOOR?

WOULD YOU RATHER...

SUFFER FROM SPONTANEOUS SHOUTING

OR

UNPREDICTABLE FAINTING SPELLS?

DRINK MILK LIKE A CAT BY LICKING A BOWL OF MILK

OR

CLEAN YOURSELF BY LICKING LIKE A CAT?

WOULD YOU RATHER...

HAVE THE HEAD OF
A RABBIT

OR

THE BODY OF A RABBIT?

EAT YOUR FAVORITE MEAL FOR
EVERY MEAL FOR THE
REST OF YOUR LIFE

OR

NEVER BE ABLE TO EAT YOUR
FAVORITE MEAL AGAIN?

WOULD YOU RATHER...

HAVE PENGUIN FLIPPERS FOR ARMS

OR

CRAB LEGS?

BE THE FIRST PERSON TO EXPLORE A PLANET

OR

BE THE INVENTOR OF A DRUG THAT CURES A DEADLY DISEASE?

WOULD YOU RATHER...

HAVE A MAGICAL FLYING CARPET

OR

A CAR THAT CAN FLY?

BE COMPLETELY ALONE FOR 5 YEARS

OR

CONSTANTLY BE SURROUNDED BY PEOPLE AND NEVER BE ALONE FOR 5 YEARS?

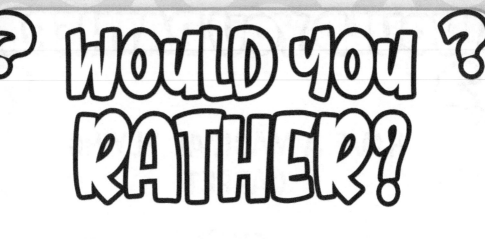

WOULD YOU RATHER?

EWW! YUCK! GROSS!

This way to crazy, ridiculous and downright hilarious 'Would You Rathers?!'

WARNING!

These are Eww! These are Yuck! These are Gross! And they are really funny! Laughter awaits!

WOULD YOU RATHER...

HAVE TO WEAR SECOND HAND UNDERWEAR

OR

USE A SECOND HAND TOOTH BRUSH?

PERFORM A TRAPEZE ROUTINE WHILE FARTING THE ENTIRE TIME

OR

RUN DOWN A STREET SHOUTING LOUDLY WEARING A GIANT DIAPER?

WOULD YOU RATHER...

HAVE A MONKEY THROW ITS POO AT YOU

OR

HAVE A MONKEY TRY TO FART AT YOU?

AN ELDERLY WOMAN FART ON YOUR HEAD

OR

YOU FART ON AN ELDERLY WOMAN'S HEAD?

WOULD YOU RATHER...

BE ABLE TO CONTROL THE SOUND OF YOUR FART SO IT SOUNDS LIKE A DOG BARKING

OR

A LION ROARING?

DROP YOUR PHONE IN A 40 GALLON DRUM OF SNOT

OR

PERFORM SWEET TRICKS ON A SKATEBOARD WEARING A USED DIAPER AS A HELMET?

WOULD YOU RATHER...

SWIM IN A RIVER OF HIPPOPOTAMUS WEE

OR

CANNONBALL INTO A POOL OF SNOT?

MARRY SOMEONE WHO IS GORGEOUS BUT SMELLS REALLY BAD

OR

MARRY SOMEONE WHO IS UNATTRACTIVE BUT SMELLS INCREDIBLY GOOD?

WOULD YOU RATHER...

BURP LOUDLY EVERY TIME YOU TALKED TO YOUR CRUSH

OR

FART LOUDLY EVERYTIME YOU KISSED SOMEONE?

EAT 16 LIVE COCKROACHES WHOLE

OR

EAT A BOOGER THE SIZE OF A GUMBALL?

WOULD YOU RATHER...

EAT A SMALL BOWL OF FRIED ANTS

OR

LICK A LIVING SNAIL?

SUCK THE EYEBALL OUT OF A DEAD FISH

OR

A DEAD RAT?

WOULD YOU RATHER...

POP YOUR FRIEND'S PIMPLE
AND LICK THE PUS

OR

YOUR FRIEND POP YOUR PIMPLE
AND LICK YOUR PUS?

DRINK SNOT JUICE WITH
YOUR BREAKFAST

OR

WATCH YOUR FAMILY HAVE A
FART COMPETITION IN FRONT OF
YOUR TEACHER?

WOULD YOU RATHER...

HAVE TO FART LOUDLY EVERY TIME YOU HAVE A SERIOUS CONVERSATION

OR

BURP AFTER EVERY KISS?

WAX AN OLD LADY'S LEG HAIR

OR

PLUCK AN OLD MAN'S EAR HAIR?

WOULD YOU RATHER...

EAT A BIG MAC YOU FOUND IN A GARBAGE BIN

OR

A CHOCOLATE BAR YOU FOUND IN A MUDDY PUDDLE?

WEAR THE SHIRT YOU'RE CURRENTLY WEARING FOR A MONTH

OR

THE UNDERWEAR THAT YOU'RE CURRENTLY WEARING FOR A WEEK?

WOULD YOU RATHER...

HAVE A WEIRD DISEASE WHERE SMELLY GREEN PUS COMES OUT OF YOUR NOSE

OR

OUT OF YOUR EARS?

EAT FRENCH FRIES THAT HAD FALLEN INTO THE TOILET

OR

REMOVE A SOGGY BAND AID FROM AN OLD MAN'S FOOT USING ONLY YOUR TEETH?

THANKS A BUNCH!

For reading our book!
We hope you have enjoyed these
'WOULD YOU RATHER?'
scenarios as much as we did as we were
putting this book together.
If you could possibly leave a review of our
book we would really appreciate it. ☺

To see all our latest books or leave a review
just go to
RatherFunnyPress.com
Once again, thanks so much for reading!

P.S. If you enjoyed the bonus chapter,
EWW! YUCK! GROSS!
you can always check out our brand new book,

WOULD YOU RATHER?
EWW! YUCK! GROSS!
for hundreds of brand new, crazy and ridiculous
scenarios that are sure to get the kids rolling on the
floor with laughter!
Just go to:
RatherFunnyPress.com
Thanks again! ☺

YOUR FREE SURPRISE GIFT!

HILARIOUS JOKES FOR CLEVER KIDS!

RATHER FUNNY PRESS

To grab your free copy of this brand new, hilarious Joke Book, just go to:

go.RatherFunnyPress.com

Enjoy!

RatherFunnyPress.com

Made in the USA
Monee, IL
24 October 2022

16421672R00063